Let's Light Up

with

ROOMIE!

A Southeastern Primer for Little Lions

Erin Moore Cowser

illustrated by **Taylor Freshley**

Have you walked around Friendship Oak
and played under its branches?

Dedicated to my dear Eliza Kate...
and Roomie, her "personal pet"

- Erin Moore Cowser

www.mascotbooks.com

Let's Lion Up With Roomie!-A Southeastern Primer for Little Lions

For more information, please contact:
Mascot Books
560 Herndon Parkway #120
Herndon, VA 20170
info@mascotbooks.com

CPSIA Code: PRT0814A
ISBN-13: 9781620867150

Printed in the United States

Have you seen the bright azaleas
while strolling across our campus?

Have you cheered in Strawberry Stadium
where Champion Lions play?

**Have you heard the crack of the bats
at The Pat on sunny game days?**

**Have you seen the Lions dunk the ball
and make some awesome moves?**

**Have you read *The Lion's Roar*
to get our campus news?**

**Have you eaten Gumbo YaYa's gumbo
and Strawberry Jubilee cake?**

Have you danced along with the Lionettes
or helped cheerleaders' pompons shake?

Have you caught beads along the route
while watching the Homecoming Parade?

Have you worn a golden mum to the Homecoming Game?

Have you tailgated in Friendship Circle
and found your brick with your name?

Have you cruised through the Student Union and proudly worn green and gold?

"We hail Thee now Southeastern,
For Thee we'll always stand.
Thy eager sons and daughters form one united band.
We'll sing thy praises ever, from sea to shining sea,
And love Thee Alma Mater,
Thru all eternity."

By Ruth Smith
Arr: Ralph R. Pottle

Have you sung our alma mater
with "eager sons and daughters" told?

If you roar as loud as Roomie can do,
they'll know you're a Lion, through and through!

ABOUT THE AUTHOR

As executive director of public and governmental affairs for Southeastern Louisiana University, Erin Moore Cowser has the privilege of representing the third largest university in Louisiana in both legislative and public arenas. With a bachelor's degree in mass communication from LSU and a master's degree in organizational communication from Southeastern, Erin has always enjoyed words – speaking them, reading them, and writing them. Her advocacy work has earned accolades, and her volunteer service has garnered awards and applause. Most importantly, however, she has the esteemed honor of being Eliza Kate's mommy.